MICK FOLEY'S

CHRISTMAS CHAOS

FOR ANTONIO FREITAS—
THE BOY FROM LAWRENCE, MASS.

The snow, it fell quite softly on this brisk December night.
The stars shone oh so brightly and they bathed the ground with light.
The evergreens swayed tall and proud in the winter breeze,
The snowcapped branches made the pines look like giant Christmas trees.

Yuletide music filled the air, faint at first, then clearer.
Could that be it, up ahead—Santa's castle growing nearer?
It truly was an awesome sight, but harder to believe
Was knowing it was just one week till—finally—Christmas Eve.

For Christmas is a magic time, a time for magic plans.
The trees, the stars, the glistening snow—it seemed a wonderland.
But sometimes things aren't what they seem, and looks can sure deceive,
For the scene inside the castle's walls was too much to believe.

The elves were running everywhere—they were loud and brash and rude,
And Tommy Top, the tallest elf, was running in the nude.
The elves were throwing toys and games, and to make things even worse,
Billy Bop, the smallest elf, was teaching them to curse.

Santa called, "Don't say bad words, I don't want to hear it.
And tiny little naked elves are not the Christmas spirit!
Put on your elf pants, Tommy Top—I don't want a naked elf.
You used to care about kids' toys, not just about yourself."

"Hey, Santa Claus," yelled Tommy Top, "let me show you a neat trick!"
Then Tommy Top, he turned around, and—my goodness—mooned Saint Nick.
Santa shook his head in shame, he knew not what to do,
And while the elves were cracking up, Billy Bop burst through.

"Hey, fatso!" yelled the tiny elf. "We're not going back to work!
And you can't make us, no you can't, you *bleep bleep bleep bleep* jerk!"
Old Santa turned his back real quick, but Tommy caught a peek—
A single tear left Santa's eye and rolled down his rosy cheek.

When Santa left the naughty elves, Billy slammed the door.
Then all the elves sat 'round the set and turned on *Raw Is War.*
Santa stumbled down the hall, his big heart clearly breaking.
"How can we have Christmas Day if the elves give up toy making?"

Saint Nick staggered up the stairs to talk with Mrs. Claus,
But as he reached the mirror, he simply had to pause.
"Maybe it's my suit," he thought as he wiped away his tears.
"I haven't changed the way I look in over ninety years.

"This beard will be the first to go, and then this old red suit,
I'll buy myself some cool new shoes, and lose these dull black boots.
And then I'll buy some fancy chains, like that wrestler named Too Hotty."
Then poor Santa took a look at his plump and dumpy body.

His butt looked like Rikishi's did, and Santa did believe
It may have been those million cookies he ate last Christmas Eve.
He had never felt this sad in all his jolly life,
So he opened up his bedroom door and told his loving wife.

But Mrs. Claus heard not a word, at the TV she was looking
She was focused on The Rock, and tried to smell what he was cooking.
Then finally old Mrs. Claus turned and said, "Come back,
In an hour, maybe two, up next is Cactus Jack."

"The Hardcore Legend!" Santa yelled, for a moment sounding jolly.
"To me, he's still the Hardcore Champ, not Crash or Hardcore Holly.
I'll tell you what"—old Santa laughed—"those wrestlers may be fakers,
But that cell match sure looked real, when he wrestled Undertaker."

Then Santa told about it all, the moon, the curse, the laughter.
Mrs. Claus said, "*Raw* is on, can't you tell me after?"
When Santa left, the missus yelled, "I don't want to be a pain, dear,
But if it's problems that you've got, go and tell the reindeer."

Mrs. Claus sure was right, for when Santa needed fixin',
Nothing made him bounce right back like a heart-to-heart with Vixen.
But Santa could not find the deer, though he searched both near and far,
Until Saint Nick heard grunts and groans from out behind the barn.

Santa walked around the barn, and to his startled eyes appeared
The sight of Rudolph being kicked by seven of his deer.
All the deer were there but one, then Santa saw the roof,
As Cupid nailed poor Rudolph's nose with a People's Hoof.

"Now stop it!" yelled old Santa Claus. "You all must stop this beating!
Just look at poor old Rudolph, his big red nose is bleeding."
"It's not our fault," old Donner yelled. "Please let me explain.
We all think that Rudolph is a great big giant pain."

"He surely is," said Blitzen, "he's got the biggest head."
"That's the truth," cried Comet, "and I'm sure glad he bled!"
"Comet's right," called Dasher. "He walks as if he thinks
That all his reindeer droppings really do not stink."

"All of you," yelled Santa, "are being pains in Santa's neck.
Ganging up on Rudolph, as if you've joined DX."
"Yeah," the bleeding Rudolph yelled, "those charges are so phony.
Rudy says those other deer are a bunch of big jabronis.

"They're jealous of old Rudy—his cash, his does, his fame.
The kids all cheer for Rudy and don't know *their* reindeer names.
Rudy has a million fans and those guys don't have any.
Rudy's toys sell out in stores; *theirs* don't draw a penny."

*S*anta Claus was shaking now, and then he started cursin'.
"I hate it when that *bleep bleep* deer starts talking in third person.
I am dear old Santa Claus, the star of this whole show!
I did just fine before you came—you and your big red nose!

"And I'll be fine when you are gone, to tell you all the truth.
First I will clothesline you down, then I'll kick your tooth.
Then we'll see if you're so smart and how you really feel,
When I give you a piledriver… and I do the move for real.

"So back away, my reindeer friends, old Santa's gonna flatten 'im,
Even if his stupid song is more than triple platinum."
"Go ahead," said Rudolph, "go ahead, make Rudy's day.
Harm one hair on Rudy's head, he'll have you sent away."

"Old Claus will then go on a trip, a long and lonely journey,
When Rudy makes a single call to his law attorney.
Just think of poor old Santa Claus, inside a dingy jail,
And how will there be Christmas joy when Santa can't make bail?"

Old Santa stopped right in his tracks; he knew the deer was right.
Santa just was not prepared for bitter legal fights.
For after Rudolph's silly song topped charts across the nation,
Rudolph won the copyright through brutal litigation.

Rudolph sure had proved to be a selfish individual,
And every time his song was played he got a small residual.
For Santa Claus, it really seemed that nothing even mattered.
Father Christmas felt his heart had finally been shattered.

Santa Claus, he used to be a ripe and jolly elf,
But now he stumbled in a trance while talking to himself.
"It hurts me that I finally know, after all these years,
That Santa Claus has just run out of all his Christmas cheer.

"I sit inside these shopping malls while little girls and chaps
All rattle off long lists of toys and pee on Santa's lap.
It used to be so easy. The boys liked choo-choo trains;
The girls just wanted dollies, or a single candy cane.

"Now the lists are longer; the kids want bigger things,
CDs, TVs, VCRs, and gigantic wrestling rings.
It used to be the kids would yell 'Santa!' and they'd hug me,
But nowadays a lot of kids would just as likely mug me.

"Let me tell you," said Saint Nick, entering his castle,
"Christmastime in days like these is just a giant hassle."
"How are you?" asked Mrs. Claus as Santa walked upstairs.
"I'm not sure," Saint Nick shot back, "that you even care."

"Now, Santa Claus," the missus said, "there really is no room
For that kind of grouchy talk with Christmas coming soon."
"My mind's made up," said Santa Claus, trying not to cry,
"It doesn't seem to matter much how long or hard I try.

"I tell the children Christmastime really gets its start
With the love they carry, inside of all their hearts."
Poor Santa's face was full of pain, his eyes were filled with tears,
Then he said, "I'm sorry—there will be no trip this year."

Throughout the castle, word was spread that Santa Claus was through.
Panic struck the little elves, for what else could they do?
Tommy Top began to cry, "Without Santa, where'd I be?
Maybe with those poor sad elves, baking cookies in a tree."

Rudolph, too, had second thoughts. He was even heard to say,
"Rudy knows it's Santa who lets Rudy guide the sleigh."
Alas, it seemed to come too late, for Santa seemed depressed,
He locked himself inside his room, and all he did was rest.

Around the world, the news had spread; the children were annoyed.
If Santa was not coming, then who would bring their toys?
By the millions, letters came and toy demands were listed.
One child wanted *Al Snow's Best Matches,* though no such tape existed.

Mrs. Claus felt terrible—she felt she was the cause.

The children of the world would weep without dear Santa Claus.

"It's all my fault for being rude, so I'll do the only thing I can,

I'll call the WF and speak to Vince McMahon."

Mrs. Claus then told the tale; Vince seemed to understand:

"I'll put my wrestlers on a plane, and they will lend a hand."

The elves were shaking in their boots when the wrestlers left the plane.

One elf even peed in his pants when he saw the size of Kane.

A startled voice then whispered loud, "Oh no, I think he's seen us!"
Saint Nick yelled, "Oh yes, I have—come out of there, Val Venis!"
Then an elf named Dewey-do yelled, "Get the North Pole cops!
We caught Jerry Lawler taking toys from our toy shop."

Kurt Angle, Edge, and Jericho were yelling at each other,
When Santa finally blew his top: "I'm Santa, not your mother!
I've always been a wrestling fan, I know those moves aren't fake,
But you've ignored my only rule, 'Be good for goodness' sake.'

"Big Valbowski, I'm sad to say, you're off my 'good boys' list.
Do your best to understand, that's my wife you tried to kiss."
To the King, old Santa said, "I hope you're not surprised
When underneath your Christmas tree you find no art supplies."

"All of you should be ashamed, so I'm giving you an order:
Get on that plane and fly right back to Vince McMahon's headquarters."
The Superstars got on the plane, then vanished out of sight,
While Santa stood out in the snow, staring off into the night.

He looked up at the brightest star—and then he made a wish.
He wished to find a single child who had no selfishness.
So Santa walked up to his room and opened up the door.
He took a giant bag of mail and dumped it on the floor.

"One thousand letters," Santa guessed, "I'll read every single one,
Searching for that special child, but after that, I'm done.
If just one child shows no greed, I'll have some hope," thought Santa.
He opened the first envelope, postmarked in Atlanta.

"Hey, Santa Claus," began the kid, "this year I want plenty.
Computer games and cold hard cash, mostly tens and twenties."
All the letters seemed the same, from Portland to Kissimee.
The children sang out like a choir: "Gimme, gimme, gimme!"

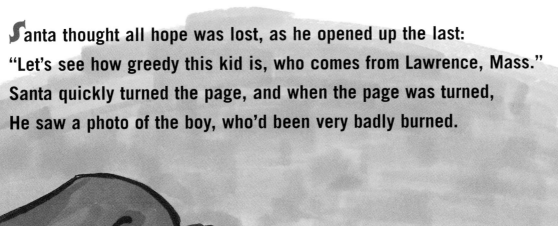

Santa thought all hope was lost, as he opened up the last:
"Let's see how greedy this kid is, who comes from Lawrence, Mass."
Santa quickly turned the page, and when the page was turned,
He saw a photo of the boy, who'd been very badly burned.

DEAR SANTA CLAUS,

I WRITE TO ASK,
PLEASE MAKE MY WISH COME
TRUE.
I DO NOT WANT A TOY THIS
YEAR—ALL I WANT IS YOU!

TO PACK YOUR BAGS AND
SPREAD GOOD CHEER AGAIN ON
CHRISTMAS EVE,
TO GIVE ALL KIDS AROUND THE
WORLD A REASON TO BELIEVE.

What pain this little boy had known, such suffering for a child.
But the thing that touched dear Santa most was the magic in his smile.
"Last year I had an accident; my life was nearly ended,
But I was given so much love while my body mended.

"The nurses—they took care of me, my mom gave gifts and parties,
I even got a chance to meet Edge, Ivory, and both Hardys.
But other kids don't have my luck—their happiness is small.
Without the thought of Santa Claus, they'd have no joy at all.

"So, Santa Claus, won't you please consider my request?
I hope that you will do what's right. I love you, you're the best."
Santa Claus put down the note; he held it to his chest.
Another tear rolled down his cheek, a tear of happiness.

"Tell the world that Christmas lives!" yelled jolly old Saint Nick.

"But if we are to make our date, we'd better move real quick."

"I will never say another curse," said tiny Billy Bop.

"And you won't see my elf butt again," promised Tommy Top.

"We know that it was we, not you, who acted like big jerks,

So all the while you've been at rest, we've been hard at work.

We made the toys for all the kids—we met all their demands.

We even made the Al Snow dolls that all the stores had banned."

The reindeer were the next to speak; they asked to be forgiven.

They even polished Santa's sleigh, the one he'd always driven.

Rudolph said, "I'm sorry, too," and to show his loyalties,

He cut the other reindeer in on half his royalties.

"I've learned my lesson, Mr. Claus, the deer and I won't fight.

And it would be an honor, sir, to guide your sleigh tonight."

Santa jumped into his sleigh and said, "Let's go, and fast!

We've got a world of kids to please; our first stop—Lawrence, Mass."

Thanks to my wife, Colette, for tolerating my year-round obsession with Christmas. To my children, Dewey and Noelle, for helping me rediscover the joys of Christmas morning and Santa's Village. To Jerry Lawler, for agreeing to become one half of the strangest tag team in literary history. To Jill "Scary Godmother" Thompson, for her talent and creativity. And to the Shriners Hospitals for Children for the miracles they make possible.

A portion of the profits from *Mick Foley's Christmas Chaos* will be contributed to the Shriners Hospitals for Children, a network of twenty-two hospitals that provide expert, no-cost orthopaedic and burn care to children under eighteen. Readers who would like to make a contribution should send a check, made payable to Shriners Hospitals for Children, to:

Office of Development
International Shrine Headquarters
2900 Rocky Point Dr.
Tampa, FL 33607-1460

HarperCollins books may be purchased for educational, business, or sales promotional use. For information please write: Special Markets Department, HarperCollins Publishers Inc., 10 East 53rd Street, New York, NY 10022.

FIRST EDITION

Library of Congress Cataloging-in-Publication Data has been applied for.

ISBN 0-06-039414-5

00 01 02 03 04   WORZ   10 9 8 7 6 5 4 3 2 1